To Mum, who is always number one!
Andrew X

For Shelagh and the Piggies
With love from Marg X

PUBLISHED BY
Wacky Bee Books
Shakespear House, 168 Lavender Hill, London, SW11 5TG, UK

ISBN: 978-1-9999033-3-6

First published in the UK 2010

This edition first published in the UK 2020

Design by David Rose

Printed and bound by ADverts, Latvia

www.wackybeebooks.com

Newt
in a
Suit

Andrew Weale

Illustrated by

Margaret Chamberlain

WACKY BEE

Here's **one** newt in a suit.

Isn't he cute!

Here are **two** flies with ties.

What handsome guys!

Now, here are **three** cockatoos
in high-heeled shoes.
That's great news!

3

But why are they so smart?
I don't know
where to start.

Oh, boy! There's more.

Four hairy apes

in brightly coloured capes.

And **five** little pigs in wigs.
Gosh! Aren't those
wigs **big!**

5

What have we got?
One newt in a suit,
two flies with ties,
three cockatoos in shoes,
four apes in capes,
five pigs in wigs.

What a treat!

But why are they so neat?

Oh, look!
There are **six** little ants
in fancy little pants.

Did I say ants?
I meant Eleph-ANTS!

7

And seven little bats.

They're wearing black top hats.

Now we're in trouble! Eight buzzing bees and they're wearing dungarees.

Oh, tell me, please!
Why are eight bees in dungarees?

And **nine** red setters in polka-dot sweaters. What could be better?

There can't be any more. Hey!
Did you hear something roar?

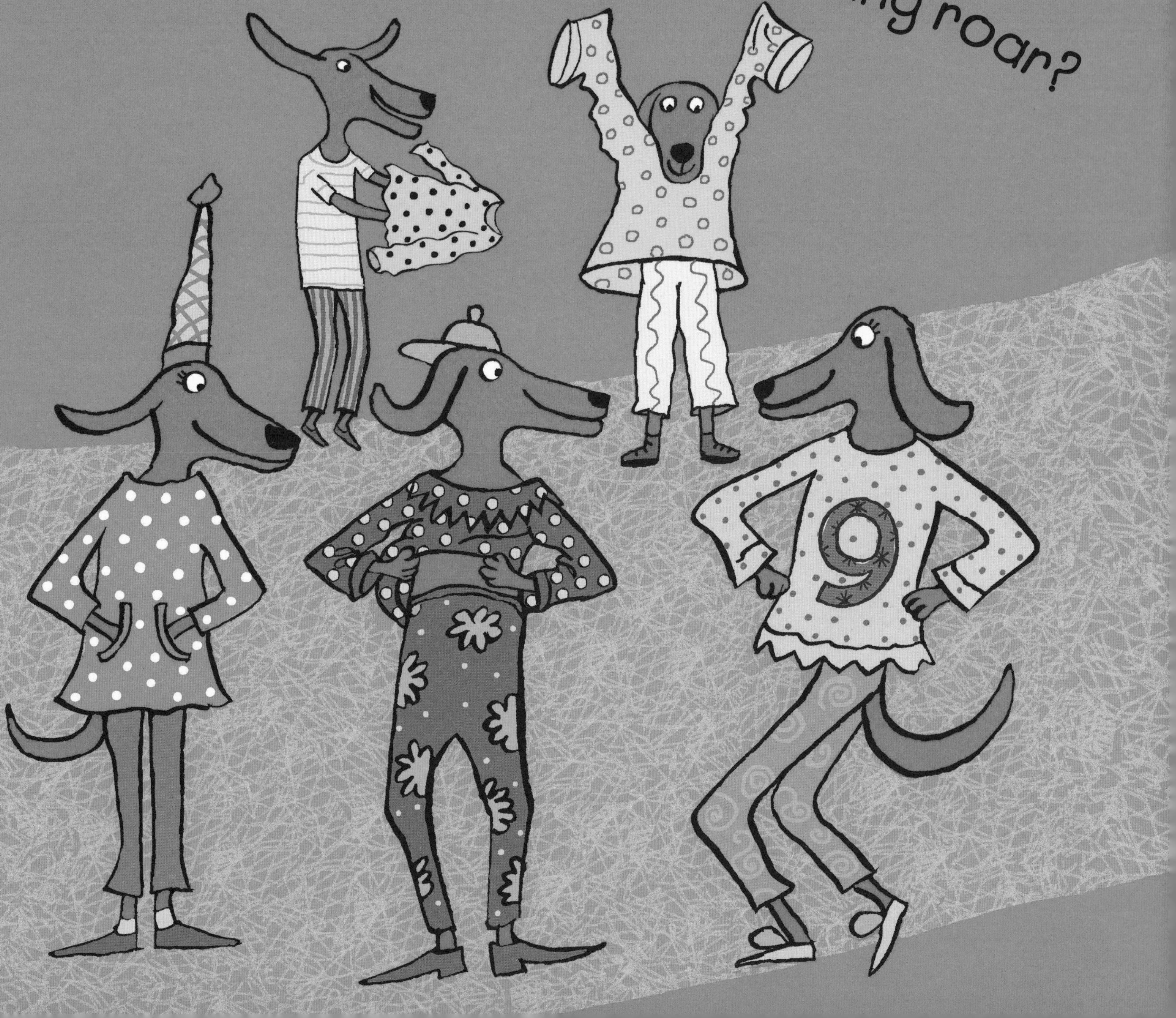

Any guesses?

What have we got?
One newt in a suit,
two flies with ties,
three cockatoos in shoes,
four apes in capes,
five pigs in wigs.
six eleph-ANTS in pants,
seven bats in hats,
eight bees in dungarees,
nine red setters in sweaters,
ten lionesses in dresses.

But where are they all going?

It's terrible not knowing!

Then, there's a BIG hip, hip hooray!

A dance, a swing and a sway!

As all the animals sing and toot...